THE
Charles
Dickens
CHILDREN'S COLLECTION

Published by Sweet Cherry Publishing Limited
Unit 36, Vulcan House,
Vulcan Road,
Leicester, LE5 3EF
United Kingdom

First published in the UK in 2020
2021 edition

2 4 6 8 10 9 7 5 3

ISBN: 978-1-78226-498-9

© Sweet Cherry Publishing

Charles Dickens: Bleak House

Based on the original story from Charles Dickens,
adapted by Philip Gooden.

Cover design by Pipi Sposito and Margot Reverdiau
Illustrations by Jon Davis

Lexile® code numerical measure L = Lexile® 630L

Guided Reading Level = Q

www.sweetcherrypublishing.com

Printed and bound in Turkey
T.IO006

Charles Dickens

BLEAK HOUSE

Sweet Cherry

ESTHER

There was once a young girl called
Esther Summerson. Esther had
never known her mother or father.
She lived with Miss Barbary, her
aunt. Miss Barbary was a horribly

strict woman, who never smiled or spoke kindly to Esther.

Esther had a lot of questions about her parents. Her aunt never answered them. She only mentioned Esther's mother once, on Esther's birthday. Miss Barbary told Esther that it would have been better if she hadn't been born. She said Esther's mother was a disgrace. 'An utter disgrace!' she shouted at Esther. 'You should forget all about your useless parents.'

Esther was miserable and
lonely. She didn't often meet other
children. Even when she did,
her aunt forbade her from
playing with them.

The only friend Esther had in the world was her doll. Sometimes she would cry herself to sleep, holding the doll to her cheek.

Esther also had a little white handkerchief. It had the letters H.B. embroidered on it in blue thread. She treasured it because she believed it once belonged to her mother.

Then, one day, everything changed.

When Esther was fourteen, her aunt died suddenly. A kind man called John Jarndyce became her guardian. He sent Esther to a boarding school. Here, for the first time in her life, Esther made friends. She was happy.

After six joyful years at school, Esther received a letter. Mr Jarndyce wanted her to come and stay at his house in the country. It was called Bleak House. Esther was worried it would live up to its name.

Mr Jarndyce was also the guardian to two other young people: Ada Clare and Richard Carstone. They were very distant members of his family. He wanted them to come to Bleak House as well.

Esther, Ada and Richard met in London, before travelling together to Mr Jarndyce's home.

Ada had thick golden hair and soft blue eyes. She was very friendly. Esther soon felt as if they had known each other for a long time.

Richard was nice, too. He was a cheerful young man who didn't take life too seriously.

It was a cold, frosty evening when the three finally arrived. The house they were travelling to lay just outside the town of St Albans. But Bleak House didn't look bleak at all. Candlelight sparkled from its windows and warmth spilled out of the front door.

Their guardian, John Jarndyce, was there to greet them. He couldn't have been more welcoming.

'Ada, my love, Esther, my dear, you are welcome here,' said Mr Jarndyce. He hugged them. 'I am so happy to see you! Richard, if I had a hand to spare, I would shake yours!'

John Jarndyce was a silver-haired man, with a face full of kindness. Like its owner, his house was warm and welcoming, and certainly *not* bleak.

But John Jarndyce explained that it had once been bleak indeed.

Bleak House had been left to John by an uncle, Tom Jarndyce. This uncle had spent his life fighting in a legal case called Jarndyce and Jarndyce. This case was many, many years old.

The Jarndyce and Jarndyce case was about a will. A long time ago, someone called Jarndyce had left a lot of money to someone else called Jarndyce. But a third person in the Jarndyce family claimed *he* ought to have the money. Then a fourth person said the same thing, and then a fifth, and a sixth, and so on …

The argument had gone on for so many years that no one could remember how it started.

Lawyers argued. Different lawyers made different arguments. Judges made judgements. Different judges made different judgements.

Everyone went round and round in circles.

The case was never-ending. But some members of the Jarndyce family still hoped that one day *they* might get the money.

Old Tom Jarndyce spent his whole life reading legal papers. He went to court again and again. The court was in the middle of London, so he travelled a lot. Meanwhile, Bleak House was falling to pieces.

The wind whistled through the cracked walls, and rain fell through the roof.

After Tom died, John Jarndyce started to put things right. He had the roof and walls repaired. He turned Bleak House into a cheerful, welcoming home.

John had a word of advice for his young wards, Ada, Richard and Esther.

'Never get involved in the Jarndyce and Jarndyce case. It is a curse, not a blessing. It will destroy your lives.'

LADY
DEDLOCK

Lady Dedlock was involved with the
Jarndyce and Jarndyce case. She and her
husband, Sir Leicester Dedlock, owned
a house in the countryside. It was much
larger and grander than Bleak House.

The only problem was that Lady Dedlock found the countryside very boring. There was nothing to do there. Especially when it was stormy and wet. The Dedlocks spent days sitting and watching

the rain. Finally, they'd had enough. 'We simply must go back to London,' moaned Lady Dedlock to her husband. 'I cannot watch another raindrop run down another windowpane – I'll go mad!'

And so, they went. Sir Leicester and Lady Dedlock travelled to their house in London. There, there was more excitement. One day, a lawyer called Mr Tulkinghorn came to see them. He had some information he wanted to show the Dedlocks. Mr Tulkinghorn was a hard-faced, sharp-nosed man. He worked on the Jarndyce and Jarndyce case. He also liked finding out secrets about the important people he worked for. Knowing their secrets gave him power over them, and he *loved* power.

It was a cold, wet, gloomy afternoon and Lady Dedlock sat on a sofa by the fire. She wasn't interested in what Mr Tulkinghorn had to say. She glanced lazily over at the papers he had brought with him.

Lady Dedlock's blood ran cold. She thought she recognised one of the handwritten papers lying on a table nearby. It couldn't be, could it? She stood up.

'Who wrote that?' she asked Mr Tulkinghorn.

'I don't know,' replied the lawyer. 'There are men paid to copy out these documents. They are called law-writers. Why do you ask, my lady?'

Lady Dedlock waved an elegant hand in the air as if to show her question didn't matter. The rings on her hand sparkled in the firelight.

She sat back down.

But the question did matter.

Mr Tulkinghorn saw how Lady Dedlock's eyes kept darting back to the paper on the table. It was obvious to Mr Tulkinghorn that Lady Dedlock recognised the handwriting.

Suddenly, the colour drained
from Lady Dedlock's face. She said
she thought she might faint. Sir
Leicester summoned Hortense, her
maid, who helped her to bed.

Lady Dedlock's husband was
worried about his wife. He didn't
notice anything odd about the way

she had acted though. He was much older than her and his sight and his hearing weren't so sharp.

As they finished their meeting, Mr Tulkinghorn couldn't help thinking about what had happened. It was clear that Lady Dedlock had a secret, and he liked collecting secrets. He decided to find out who had copied out the legal document that she was so curious about.

Mr Tulkinghorn Investigates

Mr Tulkinghorn went to the office where his legal papers were copied. He discovered that the work had been done by someone called Nemo.

Nemo?

That was strange. Nemo was the Latin word for 'nobody'.

Mr Tulkinghorn learned that Nemo lived close by. He rented a room above a junk shop. It was nighttime by now, but Mr Tulkinghorn was

determined to visit the man. Who
was he? And why had Lady Dedlock
reacted so strangely to the sight of
his handwriting?

The owner of the junk shop, Mr
Krook, told Mr Tulkinghorn that he
hardly ever saw Nemo.

'Shall I call him down, sir? I don't think he'll answer though. He might as well be dead. He keeps himself to himself, does Mr Nemo.'

'I'll go up to him then,' replied Mr Tulkinghorn.

'Second floor, sir. It's dark up there. Take this candle.'

Mr Tulkinghorn nodded and went up the narrow stairs. He reached the dark door on the second floor.

He knocked.

No answer.

He opened the door, and accidentally blew out his candle in doing so.

The small room was almost black with soot and dirt. A candle burnt low on a broken desk. Mr Tulkinghorn could also see a couple of chairs and a low bed.

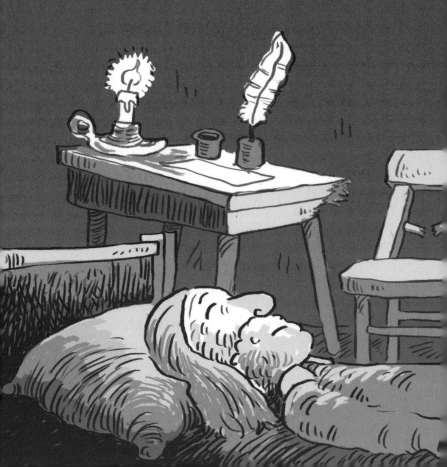

There was a man lying on the bed. He was dressed in a dirty shirt and ragged trousers, with bare feet. His hair and beard were tangled.

A couple of empty bottles lay on the floor next to the bed.

'Hello, my friend!' shouted Mr Tulkinghorn, banging his iron candlestick against the door.

The man did not move and did not answer.

Mr Tulkinghorn shouted again.

Still the man on the bed did not move, and still he did not answer.

Mr Tulkinghorn called for a doctor but it was too late.

Nemo was dead.

He was not old, but drink and poverty had hastened his death. Mr Krook, Nemo's landlord, complained that the dead man owed him six weeks' rent.

Only one person seemed sorry about Nemo's death. He was a young lad called Jo. Jo couldn't read or write and he slept on the streets. He earned a small amount of money from rich ladies, who would pay him to sweep the roads before they crossed them. Nemo had been kind to Jo. Even though he had almost no money himself, he would always give a penny or two to the boy. Now Jo sobbed. He wished he'd told Nemo just how much his help had meant.

Mr Tulkinghorn stood by and watched.

He wondered again why Lady Dedlock was so startled to see Nemo's handwriting.

Mr Tulkinghorn would have wondered even more if he had seen what happened a few weeks later.

One evening, a woman found
Jo the sweeper sitting in a shop
doorway. She asked the lad about
his friend, the man called Nemo. Jo
was a little frightened. He couldn't
see the woman's face beneath her
hat and her veil. He could only
hear her soft voice. She certainly
sounded like a lady but she was
dressed in plain clothes, like
a servant.

She said she would pay Jo to
take her to the house where Nemo
had died. Then she asked to see

the place where he was buried.
The cemetery was in a poor part of
London, behind a barred gate.

She gazed through the bars of the
gate and sighed. When she took off
her gloves to get the money from her
purse, Jo noticed how clean and small
her hands were. He noticed the fine
rings that sparkled on her fingers.
Strange kind of servant, he thought.

LADY DEDLOCK
AND ESTHER

One day, Sir Leicester and Lady
Dedlock were visiting friends in the
country. They were staying close to
Bleak House. Lady Dedlock went for
a walk with her maid, Hortense.

All at once, a violent thunderstorm
broke out. Lightning flashed, thunder
rolled and the rain came plunging down.

Luckily, there was an empty
cottage nearby. Lady Dedlock
and Hortense took shelter under

the porch of the cottage. After a
moment, three more people ran in to
join them.

It was John Jarndyce and his
wards, Ada and Esther. They too had
got caught in the storm.

Mr Jarndyce already knew Lady Dedlock. He introduced his wards to her. Lady Dedlock told Ada how pretty she was. Then, she turned to Esther. 'Have you really lost both of your parents, Miss Summerson?' she asked.

'I never knew my parents,' Esther replied.

For some reason, Esther found it difficult to speak. Her heart was beating fast and her voice sounded distant in her own ears. A strange look passed over Lady Dedlock's face. She turned and started talking to Mr Jarndyce.

All the time, Hortense watched Lady
Dedlock and Esther very carefully.

When the storm was over and
they were back in Bleak House,
Esther saw Ada glancing curiously at
her. She asked why.

'Oh, it's nothing,' said
Ada. 'It's just that I
couldn't help noticing
that you and Lady
Dedlock – well, Esther,
you look quite like her.'
Esther was so
surprised that she
almost forgot to laugh.

After all, what connection could there be between a simple young woman like herself and a grand lady?

Ada Clare quickly brushed off the idea after that. She had other things to think about. She and Richard Carstone had fallen in love and were planning to get married. John

Jarndyce approved. He was very fond of his two wards and wanted to see them happy. But he was worried about Richard.

'The trouble with Richard,' he said to Esther, 'is that he can't seem to settle down. He pins all his hopes on the idea that one day he will win money from the Jarndyce and Jarndyce case. Like my uncle Tom, he is looking forward to getting rich.'

'You don't think that will happen?' said Esther.

'The only people who make money out of the Jarndyce and Jarndyce

case are the lawyers,' muttered
John Jarndyce. 'It brings ruin to
everybody else.'

LADY DEDLOCK AND MR TULKINGHORN

In the meantime, Mr Tulkinghorn continued his investigation into the mysterious Nemo. He had made some discoveries. It was time to visit Lady Dedlock. Mr Tulkinghorn walked into the Dedlocks' house and stood to face Lady Dedlock. She was sitting in a chair by the fire. He towered over her. Mr Tulkinghorn was tall, and all dressed in black.

With his sharp nose and furrowed brow, he looked like a bird of prey.

'I have a question, my lady,' he began. Did you once know an officer in the British Army called Captain James Hawdon?'

Lady Dedlock raised her hand to her mouth. The rings on her fingers sparkled in the firelight.

She nodded.

'Captain Hawdon fell on hard times and turned to drink. In the end he became what is called a law-writer. He was so ashamed of what he'd become that he hid away and called himself Nemo.'

'I did not know that, Mr Tulkinghorn,' Lady Dedlock replied. She was trying to stay calm. But the lawyer heard a tremble in her voice.

'That was true *once*, Lady Dedlock,' he said, 'but you recognised Captain Hawdon's handwriting in the papers I showed you a few months ago. Am I wrong?' He gave her a stern look.

'I loved him,' said Lady Dedlock simply. 'I loved James Hawdon.'

Mr Tulkinghorn told her how he'd tracked down Jo the sweeper. He'd heard all about the lady with the veil who wished to see where Nemo was buried.

'I believe that lady with the veil was you, my lady. You were dressed in your maid Hortense's clothes.'

'You know everything,' said Lady Dedlock with a sigh.

Mr Tulkinghorn did know everything. He had paid Hortense to spy on Lady Dedlock.

'You had a child with Captain Hawdon,' Mr Tulkinghorn went on. 'What happened to it?'

'I was very young,' said Lady Dedlock. 'My sister, Anne Barbary, was there. I was very ill at the time, and my little girl died hours after her birth. My sister judged me for having a child without being married. She told me that I was a disgrace. We stopped talking, and now she is dead too.'

'But your daughter is alive,' said
Mr Tulkinghorn.

Lady Dedlock gasped.

'Your sister looked after her until
her death, and she lives with Mr
John Jarndyce. He is her guardian.
Her name is Esther Summerson.'

Lady Dedlock remembered meeting
Esther during the thunderstorm.

'Why are you telling me all this?'
she asked.

'Don't you think a mother ought
to know her own daughter?' said Mr
Tulkinghorn. Then a wicked glint
sparkled in his eye. 'And should

Sir Leicester Dedlock be told the secrets of your past?'

'Don't tell him,' begged Lady Dedlock. 'The shock would kill him.'

'We shall see,' said Mr Tulkinghorn.

He turned and stalked from the room like a great, evil bird of prey.

Lady Dedlock
and Esther

Esther Summerson had been very
ill. John Jarndyce and Ada had
been very worried for her. But now,
finally, she was getting better.

Esther was out walking near
Bleak House. She climbed a slope
and sat down on a bench to look
at the sunlit fields and woods. A
figure was coming towards her.
She was surprised to recognise
Lady Dedlock.

'Miss Summerson, I am afraid I have startled you,' said Lady Dedlock. 'I heard that you have been very ill.'

Lady Dedlock's face was pale. She sat down beside Esther and took her hand.

'My dear girl, I have something to tell you …' began Lady Dedlock, but she could not go on. Her eyes filled with tears. As she dabbed them away, Esther noticed that Lady Dedlock's white handkerchief had the letters H.B. embroidered on it in blue thread. It looked just like Esther's handkerchief. She always kept it because it had been her mother's.

Esther looked at Lady Dedlock, but could not see her through her own tears. She could hardly breathe.

Esther and Lady Dedlock hugged each other.

After a time, Lady Dedlock told
Esther about her father, Captain
James Hawdon. How they had
been deeply in love when they were
very young. How her family had
disapproved. How she and James
Hawdon had separated. How she
had given birth to a baby girl.

How she had been told that her daughter was dead.

Instead, the baby, Esther, had been taken away and looked after by her sister, Anne Barbary.

Lady Dedlock had been Honoria Barbary.

H.B.

Then she became Lady Dedlock, a rich woman with grand houses in the country and in London. Her husband, Sir Leicester Dedlock, was old and respectable. He loved her but he knew nothing of her past life.

She had thought her past was dead and buried. That was before she saw the handwriting which she recognised as James Hawdon's, Esther's father.

Esther could hardly take all this in.

Before Esther could respond, Lady Dedlock told her that they had to part. Something had happened. A man called Mr Tulkinghorn knew her secret, and he was going to tell her husband. Sir Leicester would never forgive her.

She didn't know what to do. She might have to leave England forever.

Esther tried to persuade her to
stay, but her mother gave her a
final hug and a final kiss. Then she
walked away.

Mr Tulkinghorn

Mr Tulkinghorn was enjoying his power. He was playing with Lady Dedlock like a cat plays with a mouse. If he revealed her past, he could ruin the lives of everyone around her. Would he do it or not? That would depend on what Lady Dedlock did.

The lawyer went to see Lady Dedlock. He wanted to scare her – if she thought he was going to reveal her secret, she would give him anything he wanted. When he arrived outside the grand

house, one of Lady Dedlock's maids
was leaving with packed bags. Mr
Tulkinghorn was furious. The Lady
was getting rid of people so he had
less spies to watch her.

He marched into the house.

'I do not approve,' he said angrily, 'of what you are doing. I see that you are trying to wriggle out of this situation.'

'Why shouldn't I?' said Lady Dedlock.

'Because now you have forced me to reveal the secret you are trying to escape,' replied Mr Tulkinghorn. 'You cannot escape me.' With that, the lawyer turned on his heels and left.

Later that night, Mr Tulkinghorn was working in his office. Hortense, Lady Dedlock's maid, had been to visit him. Now Mr Tulkinghorn had found out Lady Dedlock's secrets, he did not need

Hortense. He wasn't going to pay her any more.

She was angry.

Hortense had a fierce temper. She shouted until Mr Tulkinghorn made her leave. She stormed out of Mr Tulkinghorn's office and stamped her way downstairs.

It was a very quiet night. There was a brilliant moon. Its light turned the church steeples and rooftops of London into silver.

If you had been walking outside Mr Tulkinghorn's office just before ten o'clock that night, you would

have heard the BANG of a gun being
fired. And if you had opened the
door and walked up the stairs to
Mr Tulkinghorn's office you would
not have seen him at his desk. He lay
face down on the floor. He had been
shot straight through the heart.

MR BUCKET
INVESTIGATES

There was a police inspector in London named Bucket. It was a rather strange name but it suited the inspector. He was solid and round, just like a bucket, and he liked to scoop up pieces of information.

Inspector Bucket was investigating the murder of Mr Tulkinghorn.

Some unknown person had sent him a letter. It said: 'Lady Dedlock, murderer'.

But Inspector Bucket didn't believe everything he saw or read. He thought very carefully about things.

He visited Sir Leicester Dedlock, because Mr Tulkinghorn had been Sir Leicester's lawyer. Inspector Bucket told Sir Leicester everything he'd found out about his wife's past. How she'd been in love with a young captain. How she'd had

a baby without being married, and
how she'd believed her child was
dead. Sir Leicester was horrified
to hear how much his wife had

suffered. And now she was gone. She had run away.

Inspector Bucket thought for a while. That was suspicious. Perhaps Lady Dedlock *was* the murderer.

Then Inspector Bucket interviewed Hortense, Lady Dedlock's former maid.

Hortense admitted that she knew Mr Tulkinghorn, but did not say he'd paid her to spy on her mistress. Inspector Bucket noticed that Hortense grew angry when she mentioned Mr Tulkinghorn.

The gunshot that had killed Mr Tulkinghorn had been loud enough to

start dogs barking. It was also loud enough to make a few neighbours look out of their windows.

Some of them saw a figure slipping through the shadows. A tall woman.

Lady Dedlock was a tall woman.
But then so was Hortense.

The inspector had the maid's room
searched. There, the policeman found
two more letters. Both of them said,
'Lady Dedlock, murderer'. Just like
the one at Mr Tulkinghorn's office.

Inspector Bucket arrested Hortense. She quickly admitted that she had murdered Mr Tulkinghorn. She had killed the lawyer after an argument over money. Afterwards, she threw the pistol in the river and tried to

make Lady Dedlock look guilty.

But where was Lady Dedlock?

Esther Summerson and Inspector Bucket began to search for her. Sir Leicester was too upset to join them. Lady Dedlock shouldn't have worried. Her husband was not angry when he heard her secrets. He loved Lady Deadlock dearly and wanted her back.

Esther, too, was desperate to see her new-found mother.

But it was not to be.

When they found Lady Dedlock, she was lying by the gate of the poor people's cemetery. The place where her first love, Captain James Hawdon, was buried. Her arm was wrapped round an iron bar as if she had been trying to get through to join him.

Esther's eyes filled with tears. Her mother, Lady Deadlock, was dead.

THE END OF JARNDYCE AND JARNDYCE

Life carried on, and one day it brought the news that the Jarndyce and Jarndyce case was finally finished. It had been going on for so long that no one had expected it ever to end. Now, finally, it was over.

As it happened, Esther, Ada, Richard and Mr Jarndyce were there to see the end. Richard had gone against John Jarndyce's warning and become involved in the case. His health suffered, and he grew pale and thin. His friends worried a lot about him.

One morning, they all went to the courthouse in London. As they arrived, they were met by a huge crowd. There were a lot of lawyers with wigs on. They were all in a good mood, chatting and joking.

'What's going on?' John Jarndyce asked one of the lawyers.

'Haven't you heard?' he answered. 'It's Jarndyce and Jarndyce.'

'What about Jarndyce and Jarndyce?' said Richard eagerly. His eyes shone. His voice was hoarse.

'Why, it's over,' said another lawyer.

'All finished,' said a third.

'What's the judgement?' said Richard.

'There's no judgement.'

'Why not?' asked Mr Jarndyce.

By now, more people were streaming out of the courthouse.

They were carting out great bundles of paper. Bags of paper, sacks of paper, boxes of paper.

'There is no money left,' said one of the lawyers, laughing. 'It's all gone.'

'Gone where?' said Ada.

'Well,' said the lawyer, 'It costs money to produce all this paper and to pay people like us, you know.'

'And now it's all gone,' said John Jarndyce.

For many, many years the case of Jarndyce and Jarndyce had taken over people's lives. And sometimes it had ruined them. Richard had been saved in time.

With the court case gone, Richard could move on

with his life. Soon, he and Ada were
married with a baby boy.

Esther went on to have a happy life too. She got married to a man that she loved and had children. She had met Lady Dedlock only twice, but she kept the memory of her in her heart. And she always carried with her the white handkerchief. It was thin and faded now but the corner still had the letters H.B. on it.

Her mother's initials.

Charles Dickens

Charles Dickens was born in Portsmouth in 1812. Like many of the characters he wrote about, his family were poor and his childhood was difficult. As an adult, he became known around the world for his books. He is remembered as one of the most important writers of his time.

To download Charles Dickens activities, please visit
www.sweetcherrypublishing.com/resources